For my mother - the writer in the family.

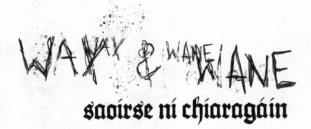

WAX & WANE

saoirse ní chiaragáin

Filthy Loot

filthyloot.com

"Don't yet rejoice in his defeat, you men! Although the world stood up and stopped the bastard, the bitch that bore him is in heat again."

- Bertolt Brecht

i: new

CORMAC

My father was a good man. He continued to be a good man, in an environment that made virtue ever harder to maintain, until his death. This life will not grant me the same grace.

The bus is late. Either that or it was early, and I already missed it, having lost precious minutes to scrambling about the house and upturning every cushion and knick-knack in the search for coins. I still ended up with less than was needed for fare, but I've found that if you drop enough shrapnel in the box when boarding, the driver doesn't even notice. Doesn't care.

It can't have always been like this. My father would never have been late when driving this route. Back then there were consequences for this sort of thing. Not just for drivers, but for everyone. You had your job and you did it right. And we were, I believe, all the better for it. Kept in line. Something today's gurriers could learn from, if you ask me.

Some days now the bus doesn't even show up. I don't know what's become of this country at all.

The rain started almost as soon as I'd left the house, and has now mostly soaked through my denim jacket. There's a chill to the air as well. I'd better not get sick. Ailbhe will get at me for not wearing something more sensible, not bringing an umbrella, but that's Ailbhe for you. She's a good woman, very nurturing. A rare breed in this day and age. I don't think I realized quite how lucky I was when I married her, how sought-after women of her kind are.

The bus arrives at last and I take a quiet joy in knowing I'm not paying the full fare. It's still more than they deserve, the bastards. Making decent people late, waiting in the rain for them to show up. Shower of wankers, the lot of them. And of course he's foreign as well, the driver. Some queer accent, has to be Eastern European. You can't move for them these days, they're everywhere. Poles, mostly. Lots of Latvians though, too. Estonians, Moldovans, Romanians. They have their own shops and everything, absolutely no effort to assimilate.

I take a seat on the upper deck, at the front. The windows are frosted with condensation, all the mingling breaths of the passengers assaulting the cold glass. The rain is really coming down now. Traffic will be bad as a result, I don't doubt it. This country. You'd think with the amount of rain we get, we'd all know how to drive better in it. I'll be late. Late for the first meeting, that won't look good. It's important to make a good first impression. It doesn't look like I'll have that luxury now.

The Irish word for wolf is *Mac Tíre*. It directly translates as "son of the country" or "son of the land". No more wolves here anymore, though. Like all the best things about Ireland, they were killed off by the Brits. Rendered extinct. Now the rest of us are in danger of becoming extinct too, it seems. A dying breed in our own nation. Jesus wept.

I thought I was the only one who cared about these things. I've tried to talk to Ailbhe about it, but she doesn't grasp the urgency of it. Doesn't see the harm. She thinks Ireland can only be improved by the hordes entering, as though we've ever benefited from foreign invaders. She thinks I'm being ridiculous. She'll be singing a different tune once we're under Sharia Law. She doesn't see that I'm really worried about her, and what this all means for the good women of Ireland and everything they've fought for.

Ailbhe's a smart woman. Certainly smarter than most women. Unlike me, she actually went to college. But because of this there are times I feel as though she condescends to me, patronizes me.

"There are more things in heaven and Earth, Horatio, than are dreamt of in your philosophy," I tell her. Partially to show off, to show her that even an aul gobshite like me can quote the Bard. But also because it's true. There's things you can't learn in college, won't learn. Sure colleges are all run by Marxists, and anything that doesn't toe the ideological line is thrown on the scrap heap. Independent learning is important, then. You've got to do your own research.

That's how I found the Mic Tíre - sons of the country, sons of the land. By doing my own research. I'd been looking for statistics on immigration and sexual assault. To show Ailbhe, to get her to understand. That's when I found a link to their forum. I must've stayed on it all night. It was like reading my own thoughts, typed out by dozens of other men from all over Ireland. And the relief! You don't know how lost you feel, how adrift and alienated, until you find your kin.

This is how we're supposed to feel, all the time. This is how the Ireland of old was, when we were divided into tuathaigh. Rival clans, ruled fairly and with purpose. It's ancient, tribal. It's natural. You can deny it all you like, but the modern way of life goes against all human instinct. And if you don't feel it yet, you will. When you find your kin, as I have, you'll feel it in your very marrow. There's no going back after that.

I despair for my father, because good as he had it, he didn't know this kind of brotherhood. This kind of unity. And surely this is what we've been striving towards since the Easter Rising. This is the Ireland that the revolutionaries wanted to forge. All of them, excluding that Scot Connolly, who'd no business being here in the first place. Ireland for the Irish. That was the promise. How those same revolutionaries would beat their chests in anguish if they could see the state of the place now.

The phone buzzes in my jacket pocket. I pull it out, fingers damp from the wet cloth. It's Ailbhe ringing. Gearing up for a row, I bet. I let it ring out. It's easier to talk her down in person, and I don't need everyone on the bus knowing our business. She'll be wound up over the money. Stupid banking apps, I always forget they notify you over everything. Better to ask forgiveness than permission, though, that's what I say. And the membership fee for the Mic Tíre wasn't even much, just a couple of hundred quid. She'll see, in time, that it's an investment. An investment in our future, in our country. I'll make her understand.

She doesn't bother to leave a message and I'm glad of it. Not that I'd have listened to it anyway. A strange fear seeds in my chest a moment, the thought that she could have been calling about Mam, but it doesn't take root. If it was about Mam she'd call again, be calling non-stop. It's just the money, and that can easily be forgiven and forgotten. Especially after I tell her about the first meeting.

I'm already giddy, that mixture of excitement and nerves you'd get as a boy before a match. The bus passes Heuston Station and we inch our way onto the quays. The rain is letting up at last, grey clouds parting just enough for some light to stream through and dry patches of wet concrete. As if Dublin knows, as though the city is opening itself up for me to meet my people.

AILBHE

Why can't he ever answer his fucking phone?

I sit on the stairs and run a hand through my hair, shaking it out of the ponytail that's kept it in place all day. It's too tight, I can feel a headache forming at my temples. I open the banking app again, staring at it as though it will change under the force of my glare. Like the money will magically reappear.

The point of having a joint account was that we'd both be paying into it. Not that I blame Cormac for losing his job. He wasn't the only casualty of the recession, it wasn't his fault. And he did try, at first, to find something else. He'd wake up with my alarm, get the kettle on and make the tea. We'd chat over breakfast, starting our days together like we had when he was working. He was optimistic. It was good. Wasn't it? The chats and the routine, it had been good. And as soon as I was out of the house and on my way to work, he'd launch into his

15

job hunt. I lost track of all the emails and applications he sent. He made job-seeking a full-time job, it was so admirable.

Then Des passed. I'd never seen Cormac so cut up. I pocket the phone, the tension in my gut dissolving somewhat at the thought of poor Des. Through the bars of the bannisters, I can see the sun flooding the kitchen, still full of memories, little knick-knacks squirrelled away in cupboards. So lived-in, yet achingly quiet now.

Of course losing a parent is hard. I lost my own father in my teens and it's not something you ever recover from, not fully. But Cormac just disappeared into himself. I suppose it made it harder, us all living under the same roof. We'd become so mixed up in the rhythms of one another's lives, myself, Cormac, Des and Jacinta.

The plan had been to live with his parents until we could save enough for a deposit. But then the recession. Then Des. It all feels like it was another life.

The deposit fund is long gone. With Des passed and Cormac's mam, Jacinta, bedridden, mortgage payments fell to us. I suppose we did, in a way, become homeowners. Wishes always get warped somehow, don't they?

I would never begrudge Cormac the money. Not under normal circumstances. But Christ, it was a lot. What's he even spending four hundred euro on? I wouldn't mind, only it's money that we needed for the car. The tax isn't paid up on it and the brakes have gone dodgy. Taking the bus to work and back means an added two hours on my commute each day, thanks to the sparse scheduling and outrageous traffic. I can't even complain about it anymore because Cormac just gets up on his soapbox, uses it as an excuse to launch into his laundry list of all the ills of Ireland. I'm too tired to listen lately.

He wasn't always like this. At least, that's what I

tell myself. I never would have married the man he is today. Would I have even entertained a conversation with him? I've spent months telling myself that it's the grief. That he's grasping desperately for some semblance of control, but I wonder if I'm just letting him off the hook. Some of the things he comes out with are so awful. I never knew he had so much hatred in him. It's like something in him died along with Des and has been rotting ever since, spewing its foul muck into the air.

It's quiet. I wonder if Jacinta is sleeping. She doesn't make much noise at the best of times though, God love her. She'd already started forgetting things long before Des died. But she was mobile then, and still largely herself. Alzheimer's is an awful thing, isn't it? How it eats away at a person. It's scary to think how fragile we are. How we can just be spirited away by a disease like that. At least she's peaceful. I think. In the early days, I know she was frightened. How could you not be? But as more and more of her fell away, the part of her that was afraid disappeared.

I climb the stairs to check in on her. I can't just take it for granted that Cormac tended to her before leaving. And where is he anyway? A knot forms in my stomach, wondering about his absence and the withdrawal from the joint account. Has he left me? Would he leave me? The fear passes as soon as it's arrived and I have to laugh.

Good luck to you, I think. *You wouldn't get very far without me paying your way.*

It's unfair, and I would never say it aloud, but I can't deny that it's true. He stopped drawing the dole weeks ago. After a few weeks of no-shows, they freeze payment. To get it up and running again you have to go to your local Department of Social Protection and explain why you stopped withdrawing the funds, and hope that they'll take sympathy. Cormac hasn't done that though. Reckons it's too much effort. Much easier to stay online all day chatting with his internet friends and living off his wife's wages.

I did worry, at first, that he was having an affair. All that time spent in front of the computer, barely able to tear his eyes away from the screen. I'd wake up some nights to an empty bed. He'd be downstairs, sat in the dark, only the pale light of the laptop screen illuminating the sitting room. I wonder now if any other woman would even have him.

Jacinta is awake when I crack open the door and look in at her. She still has the master bedroom. It didn't seem right to move her, given her condition, even with Des gone. Though, of course, this means that Cormac and I are resigned to his childhood bedroom. There's just enough space to fit a double bed, but that takes up most of the room. We keep our clothes in two chests of drawers on the landing, which make the narrow stretch of walkway all the more difficult to navigate.

"Howye Jacinta," I say, and she moans in response.

It's a happy moan, though, light. She's in good form.

I walk over to her bed and am thankful when I'm not assaulted by any stench. She needs so much care of late. She can't make it to the bathroom on her own, and there have been so many accidents that we've had to start dressing her in adult nappies. If she was still all there, I'm sure she'd feel humiliated. She was always such a proud woman. I suppose it's some comfort that the dignity died with the fear.

"Where's that son of yours?" I ask her. "Out gallivanting, is he?"

Cormac doesn't speak to her. Says he doesn't see the point, now that she can't respond. I think it's important, though. Maybe it keeps a spark lit in there. Even if it doesn't, she's still a person. Still deserves to be included, to know the day-to-day goings-on. She's still part of the family.

I pull back the net curtain of the window to check the front garden. It's overgrown, but I've given up telling Cormac to mow it. One of these days, by some miracle, I'll have the energy to tend to it on the weekend. Until then it's lush with nettles and tall grass, the last of the summer's butterflies dipping in and out of its thick greenery. I notice that the dogs are back. Two of them, same as before. Strays, I think. Nobody around here will claim them, anyway. Plus they're rangy, don't look fed. They've knocked our bin over I don't know how many times, looking for scraps.

The sound they make at night is dreadful. All that howling.

ii: waxing crescent

CORMAC

Can't remember where I buried the damn thing. We should've marked it with something. A wooden cross or a few rocks. Had a proper burial. But Ailbhe was too distraught at the time and I thought it best to just get it over with, so she wouldn't have to look at the poor thing.

Silly aul cat. It was Ailbhe's cat, really. Already had it when I met her. And she babied that thing like you'd never believe. Only the best food, couldn't just waltz into a supermarket and pick up any run of the mill kibble for this cat. I thought it was daft, but who was I to argue? Wasn't my cat.

I thought she'd never stop crying when it died. I've seen Ailbhe cry plenty of times. Women cry, it's what they do. But not like that. I'd expected her to wail, crumple in on herself like you see people do in movies. She didn't. She just got very quiet. I think she tried to avoid me. We were never in the same

25

room long. But when we were, when I did see her, the tears were just streaming down her face. A constant cascade of them. I didn't know anyone could ever be so sad over a cat.

I kick the loosened dirt with my shoe. I keep expecting to see bone, but it can't be that rotted yet. It's only been a month or so. Still, I'm trying to be careful. I don't want the shovel to split it, to have to carry it to the next plot in pieces. Ailbhe thinks the stray dogs are drawn to the stink of it. That they've been sniffing around, trying to dig up the body. She's probably right. Dogs are like that. Especially when they're desperate, they'll dig up any dead thing and make a meal of it. Dead doesn't matter to dogs.

Then again, it could have been a clever ploy of Ailbhe's to get me to finally work on the garden. God knows she's been on my case about it enough. Don't know why she couldn't get out there herself, there wasn't much of a job to it. Some of the weeds had grown thick, and the lawn now looks patchy, uneven.

But the grass is short now and the land can be dug, and that's all that was needed. I think sometimes women reserve certain tasks for men. Not because they're unable to do them, but because it's all part of the dance, isn't it? They're capable, but they always need the man to take that extra step.

It's something Ailbhe will need to grow out of if we're to turn the country around. The role of women in the reclamation of Ireland was a big topic at the meeting. Ailbhe was already asleep by the time I came home. I was disappointed, but it didn't linger. Didn't bite into the bones of me like it has of late, when I've been dying to talk to her about everything. To get her to listen to the truth of our reality, engage with what's going on. No, after the meeting, I was buoyed enough. I lay, still clothed, on the bed beside her and just smiled. Smiled into the dark, feeling a hope I thought was lost to me.

There's a dark tuft of something peeking through the soil. I hunker down to get a closer look and brush the dirt away with my hands. It's the cat, right enough. I dig away at it with my hands, careful not to disturb the body much. Mad how fragile it looks, so much of the flesh festered away, the pelt clinging to the bones. How delicate. Imagine, that's how it looked all along, under the meat of it. Just a flimsy little thing, easily broken. I lift it gently from the grave, place it in the curve of the shovel to be taken around to the back.

The dogs are standing at the gate. It's open, but they don't cross the invisible threshold into the driveway. Their tails are wagging, both of them manged, the fur thinned and pale skin beneath scabbed. I can hear their high whinnies, the scent of the cat likely driving them mad. How long since either of them have eaten, I wonder?

"An bhfuil ocras oraibh?" I ask.

I've been making more of an effort of late to use my *cúpla focail*, the odd bits and pieces of Irish I still remember from school. Language is a pillar of the reclamation, according to the Mic Tíre, and I wholeheartedly agree. It is a great shame of mine that my grasp of Irish is so poor. Ailbhe, of course, is fluent. She's a teacher, she has to be. I daren't try speaking with her. She'd only correct me at every turn. I want conversation, not a lesson. It just isn't worth the hassle. In the meantime I speak it to myself. To the dogs.

Sometimes I think about putting the work in, becoming fluent. I'll say nothing to Ailbhe. And then one day she'll say something in Irish. Mutter to herself the way she often does, thinking I don't understand. But this time I will understand. And I'll correct her, or admonish her, and she'll be overcome with surprise and embarrassment.

Ailbhe never had to put the work in. Like most things in life, the language was handed to her. Her parents spoke Irish in the home, were both avid advocates for it. She doesn't know the struggle of the rest of us. The soul-deep pining for the identity we were robbed of. It used to be a point of pride, my gaeilgeoir wife. I don't take pride in it anymore. It's unbecoming for a wife to hold knowledge inaccessible to her husband.

I plod around to the back garden and the dogs follow, as though commanded. I've already picked a new burial plot. Ailbhe won't want the dogs being near it, knowing where the cat is buried, but that's no concern of mine. I'm moving the cat and that's my job done. The cat. Sure that was the beginning of all the misfortune, wasn't it?

We've not been intimate since it passed. Ireland is crying out for children, a new generation, and she won't heed the call. She knows how badly I want us to have a family. How important it is for us to keep the blood alive. Most nights Ailbhe is asleep before I am. She says she's tired from work. I can't help but feel like it's a barbed remark, reminding me that she's the breadwinner. As though I don't carry the weight of that fact in my stomach every day, sick from the shame of it. All the jobs are taken by immigrants anyway. An Irishman can't get hired in his own country now. For now, the reclamation is the work.

She says she's tired, but she's punishing me. I know it. For the cat. For the work. For my mam, and being trapped in this house. All of it. It all becomes my fault. I stab at the ground with the shovel, the dogs eyeing the prone body of the dead cat.

And there's so much I want to say. The anger in me rises and I want to spit it forth, shout it in my native tongue, and I can't. I can't and she knows it, and that gives her power over me. I fling the cat into the shallow hole and cover it with dirt. If the dogs dig it out, tear it apart, it is of no consequence to me. And let Ailbhe see it as well, let her see and think of how delicate a creature she is too, and how quickly the dogs do come sniffing.

AILBHE

I had a terrible dream.

I was pregnant, my belly swollen so far that I couldn't see my own feet. And in that strange dream logic that exists, it was growing larger with every passing minute, as though that's a normal part of pregnancy. I remember thinking that I would burst, I was so afraid. Stretch marks formed along the ballooning surface of my abdomen, and I watched in horror as the skin split along these fault lines and gave way like cracks in the earth.

Suddenly I was on my back, and my body seemed to stretch on forever. There were roads and paths along it, all shuddering and quaking and falling into the rapidly erupting fissures. I was made of so much and it all began to crumble, fall in on itself, and I realized that I was in labour. That this was childbirth.

I was alone. I hadn't noticed at first, but it became

very apparent to me, and the fear and loneliness of it shook my chest with sobs. I wanted Cormac, needed him by me, and yet was so angry. Angry that he wasn't there, that he'd gotten me in that state in the first place. There were great plumes of dust as the city that was my body collapsed and every nerve sang with pain, its resonance vibrating through my limbs. Crawling its way out of me, dragging blood and viscera in its wake, was something small and dark.

I eased up to get a closer look, my belly no longer obscuring my view, and the breath caught in my throat. It was a little dog, a puppy. Cased in an amniotic sac, its eyes closed and fogged beneath the membrane.

I haven't been sleeping well. Every night those dogs come sniffing around and howl for hours. When I do sleep, it's in fits. And the dreams are dreadful. Vivid and sickly, the howls winding their way into my subconscious from the garden below. I've tried earplugs but they don't help. Probably something to do with the frequency of the dogs' cries. Why do they keep coming back?

We'd called the ISPCA about them, had them collected and brought to a shelter. They just escaped and returned all the same. They have to be eating more than just the scraps from our bins. I don't know how they've managed to survive so long otherwise. Cormac is taking a shine to them. He needn't get any ideas. Dogs like that are too far gone, can't be domesticated. There's a meanness to them. I've told him not to touch them. I know I must sound like a scold, like I'm infantilizing him, but I'd be the one having to cart him off to hospital if he got rabies.

I stand in the kitchen and wait for the kettle to boil. I've more coffee in my system than blood these days, I'd reckon. It's all that gets me through the day. I love my job. I love teaching Junior Infants. The drama of it. The tears on the first day, the first real goodbye to mammy and daddy. The new friendships, the fall-outs. The enthusiasm. There's a shine on everything at that age. It's a joy to witness, but it takes a lot of energy.

WAX AND WANE

Some days it's a struggle to sit upright at my desk.

I pile the mound of coffee granules high upon my spoon, hoping it will be enough. Through the window I can see Cormac enter the garden, the shovel held in front of him, Jasper's poor little frame cradled in it. I turn away, I don't want to see her like that.

She was such a good cat. We didn't know she was a she until long after we'd named her Jasper, but I don't think she minded. I'd never known a more affectionate animal. She'd curl up on my lap every evening while we watched TV in the living room, stretching her head towards my mouth occasionally in anticipation of a kiss, purring loudly until she fell asleep. When I was sad, I'd bury my face in her rich, earth-scented fur and feel her warmth. Listen to her little heartbeat.

It sounds so stupid. But in a home that wasn't mine, that held none of my memories, she was something that belonged to me. She was that bit of myself, externalized, that I could turn to and feel like I was where I was meant to be. And then she was gone.

I hear a bark through the window and my pulse quickens. Cormac has let the dogs into the back. For a split second I consider rapping on the glass, shouting at him to chase them out, but I worry that by distracting him it will give the dogs a chance to grab Jasper and run off with her. He'd only say I was making a fuss anyway, that the dogs were keeping their distance and that I'd nothing to get so up in arms about.

He's been short with me lately. Terse. We haven't had sex in a month, maybe more. Not since Jasper died. For the week or two following, I just couldn't face him. I was shocked by the extent of the pain I felt. And Cormac's attempts at coercion didn't help matters, either. Not that I require any grand romantic gestures, but his favoured approach of late was to remind me of the nation's dwindling birth rates. The disastrous effects of the legalization of abortion. The influx of migrants, and the supposed genocide of indigenous Irish people. It wasn't exactly pillow talk.

I can't talk to him when he's like that. There's no getting through to him. Sometimes it feels like he views me more as a broodmare than a wife. He's started going to meetings. Sank four hundred euro of my money into membership. I was nearly sick. I've been trying to reason with him. Get him to go to couple's counselling, or even see someone on his own if he wants his space from me. I'm willing to take a step back if he'll put the work in. Anything to move past this fixation. To process this grief, or whatever it is, and come out the other end.

I drink a big gulp of my coffee. It's hot and bitter and I can feel it spark throughout my body, knocking the fog of sleep out of my brain. In the garden, Cormac covers Jasper with a thin layer of dirt. It's not enough to keep the dogs at bay. I'll have to do it myself. He slinks away, his job done, and the dogs follow. Their heads are slung low, as though they're bowing. I wonder if he's feeding them. Leaving out food while he's up all hours, coaxing them back again and again and letting them howl nightmares into my sleep.

Is he doing this to punish me? Because I won't entertain his growing bigotry, or because I won't offer myself up? Won't do my wifely duties?

I'm surprised when I find myself crying, one big salty tear falling into the coffee with a hollow plop. I chide myself, because I know I'm more tired than anything else, and that it won't be like this forever. But God, for now it's so hard and it feels like so much. And if I had that little cat I would hold her close and be comforted by the warmth of her breath, the steady beating of that small heart.

The coffee can wait. Jasper cannot. I step outside to heap more dirt upon her body, and pray the dogs don't find her.

iii: first quarter

CORMAC

There's an art to carrying pints to a table, an art I've yet to master. The froth of the heads laps about with each step, spilling over the lip of the glass and dribbling down onto my hands. But there's a cheer from the lads when I finally set them down gently onto a patch of sticky rings worn into the wood from decades of slick glasses. And it feels good to have that cheer, to be supplying a round. I don't know how long it's been since I've been out like this.

Definitely not since dad passed, anyway. He was a good man for a drink. We'd often pop down the local on a weekend, watch any aul match that happened to be on. It was less about the game and more about having somewhere to look while we spoke. Somewhere that wasn't one another's faces.

When the meeting came to a close, I was hesitant to get out of my seat. It had been a good meeting, of course. The meetings are always good. I often want to hang around afterwards, get into the meat of what was discussed, really pore over it with the rest of them. But usually they all head home fairly sharp. Wives and children at home. Me too, obviously. Not a child, but the wife. But I'm in no rush to get back to her tonight. So when the evening's agenda was all done and dusted, I was delighted to be invited a short walk away to a small pub. Quiet. Far from the crowds and their chatter, the awful bastardized twang of students, raised by American television and films. Far from the tongues clacking in all the languages of the world, like Dublin itself was ground zero for the tower of Babel's fall. A secluded place, where we could talk amongst ourselves.

We'd had a row before I left. It started because of the cat, and the new hole I'd dug for it. I found her in the garden, piling dirt on top of the dirt I'd already heaped. Asked her what the story was.

"It's not enough," said she. "The dogs can still get at it."

I rolled my eyes at her. Told that the dogs had been sat as close to the thing as she stands to me now, and they'd not made an attempt to go near it. That they don't care about the yoke, have better things to be sniffing after.

"They were probably just afraid of you," she said, returning to her task. "They'll come back when we're asleep. They're always back at night."

It shouldn't have stung me the way it did. But lately it's as though I can't do anything right for that woman. She's this high-and-mighty attitude of late that I didn't recognize in her before. When she looks at me there's a contempt to it. Unspoken, unaddressed, but naked and brazen all the same.

I must have some hang-dog expression. Must wear every bit of the row with Ailbhe in the lines of my face, because one of the lads - Liam, his name is - asks me what's up. I shrug, take a deep gulp of my stout. It's heavy, dark. Hits my empty stomach pleasurably.

"Ah y'know yourself," I say. "The missus isn't fond of me going to these meetings."

The other lads shift slightly in their seats, as though I've made them uncomfortable, said the wrong thing. It's been a long time since I've cared so deeply about the opinions of other men. I feel an adolescent anxiety reawaken in me, bubbling just beneath the stout.

"Not that that would ever stop me coming," I explain.

To cut through the tension, Liam tilts his glass towards me and winks.

"*Maith thú*," he says, disappearing into a long draw of his own pint.

Some of the others smirk. I wonder if they think less of me now. Have I made myself look like that breed of man who lives under the heel of his woman. And if I have, is it not the truth? Am I not sat here, spending Ailbhe's money on rounds, acting the big man while she sits home alone and nursing her bruises?

I hadn't meant to hit her. But she was so haughty, so strident when she carried the shovel inside and kicked off her boots. Moving with such speed and purpose. To get away from me. Be clear of me. And again I thought of how long it had been since I'd held her. Since she'd deigned to give me permission to touch her. My own wife. How she kept putting this distance between us. How nothing was enough.

I called after her. Tried to get her to stop, to slow down and face me, see me and listen to me. For once, just listen to me. And when she wouldn't stop, when she kept moving, I grabbed her wrist and spun her around to me. She was so frightened then. Looking at me like she didn't know me, like I was some stranger who showed up in her house. But it isn't her house. It's my house. The house I've lived in all my life. And in my father's absence, I'm the man of that house. Something she would do well to remember, and I told her as much.

Then the fear melted from her, seemed to drain right out of her, and she laughed. Would you believe that, she laughed.

"I don't know where this macho bullshit is coming from," she said. "But it would seem far less ridiculous if you could back it up in any way."

"I hit her," I say, to the lads I suppose, though I speak it into my pint.

The tension dissipates somewhat, some of them angling their bodies towards me again. Seán, the alpha of our chapter, drinks deeply from his glass, his expression pensive.

"That's needed, from time to time," he says, and there's a warmth to his gaze when he regards me.

"Until she is broken, until she accepts her role in the reclamation, that'll be needed."

I nod, not quite sure what to say.

"You've no children yet?" Seán asks. "She isn't pregnant?"

I shake my head, no. He mulls this over.

"You'll have to get started on that," he says. "You've cowed her now, and that's good. Get her back on side, start the work on the breeding. It might take a more gentle hand, but the repopulation is the main thing."

He's right. Ireland needs her children. The population is still lower than it was pre-famine. And so muddied now, with all the rubbish that washes up on her shores. She needs fresh blood. It's our duty to provide.

I drain my glass, the white foam clinging to the inside at an incline. Liam pats me on the back with a smile.

"Same again?" he asks, and I nod my appreciation.

Seán leans back in his chair, those warm fatherly eyes still drinking me in.

"What's your schedule like this week, Cormac?" he asks me.

Seán knows that I'm unemployed. He tells me that dedicating myself to learning, to reconnecting with our language and history, is job enough in itself. But he still asks as a sign of respect. He's the alpha but he's no tyrant. He sees me as the man I am.

"Fairly clear," I tell him. "Why?"

Liam returns with a fresh round of pints, placing mine in front of me. He hasn't spilled a single drop.

"Time to prove your worth," Seán says, raising his glass in mock-toast, his eyes closing in satisfaction as he knocks back his drink.

AILBHE

I always told myself that if he ever hit me, I'd leave. No question.

It's easy to tell yourself those things when you believe it will never happen. Not me. Not my husband. You always think you're different, don't you? Special somehow. Bad things only happen to other people. But sometimes the bad things find you too.

My own father, may he rest, hit my mother. I don't know if it was a repeated offence, or just a one-off. At any rate, I didn't learn about it until after he passed. He was dead some years when she told me. We were both drinking in her living room, the hours stretching into morning. I suppose we had been reminiscing about him. He was a great dad. I loved him very much. But as I spoke, I noticed something sour in her expression. In the low light, there was a sorrowful gleam to her eyes. And then she told me.

51

WAX AND WANE

I don't really know what to think about my father anymore. It's like he's split into two people. The father I loved, who was everything a dad should be to a child, the father who died and broke my heart. And then the father after he died. All the sins rising from the earth where we'd buried his goodness. Hanging around and poisoning his memory.

And I hated her for telling me. I know how awful that sounds, and I am ashamed of that feeling, but it's true. I understand she had to say it, had to get it outside of herself in some way. I don't believe she'd ever told another living soul. But why me? Why destroy the image of the man so thoroughly? Now my love for him feels like a betrayal. Like something wrong.

I hold a bag of frozen peas to my eye, like they do in the movies. The numb coldness of it feeds into the unreal nature of the whole thing. He'd normally be back from his meeting by now, is likely avoiding me. Not that I mind. I don't want to face him yet. Don't know what I'll say when I have to.

I have half a mind to pack a bag. Call a taxi. Book a hotel room. I don't need a plan beyond that, not for now. Just get away, leave no way for him to find me. Don't answer my phone. Close the joint account, withdraw the money. Call in sick to work. My mind is on fire, laying out each step and it all seems so easy. So doable and so necessary. I'm screaming at myself to leave, I know that it's the only right thing to do.

And yet.

And yet I can hear Jacinta moaning in her bed upstairs, distressed and insistent. I drop the bag of peas and climb the stairs, her cries growing louder. I open the door and am greeted by the smell. Fighting the urge to retch, I look at her face, at the sorrow and fear in her eyes. She can't help it. And who would care for her if I was gone? Not Cormac. Certainly not. And it's not like I can take her with me.

"It's OK, Jacinta," I say to her. Softly. Because I really do mean it.

I peel back the blankets and ready a fresh nappy. She's trembling, and I'm not sure if it's from the cold or the upset or some unknown thing, something that only exists within her and can't be spoken into the world. How lonely it must be, to be alone in your own mind like that.

"I'd never leave you," I say to her, and immediately feel foolish when I feel tears well in my eyes.

My own mother warned me against marrying Cormac. I suppose she saw something in him that I was blind to. Some echo of my father, an aspect of the man I had yet to learn. Some hidden violence. I didn't understand. Couldn't understand her insistence on spoiling this moment of happiness.

"You can't love him into someone better," she said.

But I hadn't wanted someone better. I wanted Cormac, he was enough. And he really was enough, once. We had been good, I didn't just imagine that. But like my father, there are two Cormacs. The man

I married, and the man that emerged following Des' passing.

I should have left after Jasper died. Cormac insisted that it had been an accident. That he was agitated, trying to focus on something, and that Jasper kept getting under his feet. She often cried when I was away, missed me, and wouldn't settle until I was home again. And normally Cormac could block it out, even sympathize with her. But it was too much that day, he said, and he just snapped. He only kicked her once, he said. Just to get her out of his way. A sudden, thoughtless act, he hadn't meant to do it. And he certainly hadn't meant for it to be as forceful as it was.

It was enough, though. Enough to crush her little skull. I suppose I should be thankful it was quick. She can't have suffered much.

I was so stunned when he told me. Numb, cold. I couldn't look at Jasper, her small body left in a corner of the kitchen. I let him take her to the front garden, bury her where she would later be covered by the long grass, the flowering weeds. He didn't mean it. That's what he said, and that's what I kept telling myself. That he didn't mean it, wasn't the kind of person to consciously be capable of such a thing. But I couldn't get the tears to stop falling, and I couldn't bring myself to talk to Cormac.

At night, when he crawls into bed beside me, I feel myself recoil. It's an instinctive thing, something I can't help. If I entertain the thought of him touching me, my mind flashes to Jasper. That sudden outburst, and the fury he must have felt. The weight behind that kick.

I couldn't keep him at bay forever. I dab at the swelling around my eye socket. The first time he's touched me in almost two months. By force, by fury. How can I leave? Where would I go?

Jacinta rests in a chair, freshly changed, while I

strip the sheets from the bed and fit clean ones. She should be in a home. Somewhere she'll be properly looked after. Cormac refuses, of course. Says this is her house, that she deserves to die in dignity in the home she made. But there doesn't seem to be much dignity in it.

Beyond the window, the dogs start up their howling. By the volume of it, I can tell that they're around the back. I drop the sheet to pull the curtain just to be sure. I see only the driveway, the car parked and gathering dust, reflecting the orange light of the streetlamps.

I wander to our bedroom, squeezing past the chests of drawers on the landing, crawl over our unmade bed to the window. That's when I see them. I frown, and the tears flow freely down my cheeks, stinging my bad eye on their exit. It's too late. They've already dug her up, have divided her between them. She hangs from their mouths, bathed in saliva, sparkling in the moonlight. Nothing of her is left. Goodbye, little Jasper.

iv: waxing gibbous

CORMAC

Things have been better these past few days. Ailbhe feels it too, I'm sure of it. I've *made* sure of it. Naturally, she took a great deal of talking to. She was very upset, and with good reason. I hadn't realized how hard I'd actually hit her. I came home, unsteady on my feet after the rake of pints, and stumbled up the stairs. I could see how bad the swelling was, even in the dark. Part of me worried I'd broken something, caused a fracture somewhere hidden beneath her skin.

She called in sick the next day. Didn't want the children seeing her in that state. Didn't want anyone seeing her in that state, I imagine. I apologized constantly. When I woke. When I brought her breakfast in bed, on a little tray and everything. Pulled a flower from the garden and placed it next to the plate, tried to make something romantic of it. She wouldn't budge, spent the day largely in silence. Never even left the bedroom. Most of the times I checked in on her, she was sleeping. Or, at least, appeared to be. I whispered my apologies all the same. Over and over. I'm sorry, I'm so sorry.

I told her I'd started looking for work again. That I'd contact that DSP, get my dole up and running again. I'd search for therapists, see if any had a sliding scale for payment, figure something out. Most of it was lies. Things Seán had suggested. But they were good suggestions, and they worked. Bit by bit she came out of herself, came back to me.

"I want to understand," she said. "I really do. I don't know what's prompted all this."

So I told her. Dad's death didn't help, of course, but I suppose it really began with mam's diagnosis. We all know we'll die someday. We learn that as children. If you're lucky, if you're healthy, this fact shouldn't frighten you. It's just a natural part of life. What caught me off-guard, the fear that seized upon me when mam began to lose parts of herself, was that parts of you can die before your body goes. And I don't just mean mam, and the parts of her that had died through the disease. Her memories and her thoughts, the things that made her her.

No, parts of me have died. Parts that lived only in her. Memories of my childhood, my infancy. Aspects of myself that are lost to me, inaccessible. I suppose I'd never thought of it before. How there are parts of ourselves that exist in other people, and that once they're gone, that's it. A chunk of your history is lost forever. There's no getting it back. We are, all of us, dying slowly with every death we witness, with each disease that takes hold. All of us living within one another, strengthened and made more vulnerable.

There's an old Irish proverb that goes, *"Ar scáth a chéile a mhaireann na daoine."* It means "people live in each other's shadows". There's a reason we have such a strong oral tradition. A reason why we lived in small tribes. We kept one another alive, with our words and our memories. In a way, it made us all immortal.

WAX AND WANE

We've lost that, though. The modern world hinges on the individual, at the expense of the collective.

I explained to Ailbhe that that's what I've found in the Mic Tíre. A collective, a fraternity. Something that I didn't know was missing from my life all this time. Something that keeps me alive. She tried to understand. Is still trying.

I know she'll come around. A gentle hand, that's all it takes. It's been easy, treating her kindly this past while. Easy to be kind when you're happy. And I haven't been this happy in a long time.

Seán had called me to meet him near a patch of woodland, not far from the bog of Allen in the midlands. A bastard to get to by bus, but I managed it, just about. Light was already fading when I arrived, but he seemed glad of it.

"Better to get it done under cover of dark," he said, smiling, and led me into the woods.

I don't know how long we walked for. I wasn't dressed for it, at any rate, the soles of my trainers becoming gummed up with mud and rotting leaves. As it grew darker, it became more difficult to spot the soft rises and falls of the terrain, and I found myself stumbling quite a bit. If Seán noticed, he didn't let on, striding ahead and scanning the horizon.

At last we stopped. I panted, struggling to catch my breath, while Seán regarded the spot of woods we'd found ourselves in. While I gulped at the cold air, my chest bracing with each inhalation, it suddenly occurred to me that I didn't really know this man at all. And yet here I was, in the middle of nowhere after dark, alone with him. Ailbhe didn't know where I was, had been told only that I was headed out to another meeting. I was completely at his mercy.

It was a stupid thought. I'd every reason to trust him. But I will admit that the fear lingered in me as he brought his fingers to his mouth and whistled, clear and high, the sound of it resonating throughout the trees.

For a moment, nothing happened, and we stood in silence. Then, a howl. Matching the pitch of Seán's whistle, it cut across the dark. It was joined by another, and another still. Seán turned slowly towards me, his mouth twisting into a smile. He took a step forward, his hand in his pocket.

"You've been a fine addition to the chapter, Cormac," he said.

He came closer. The howls rang out, growing louder all the time.

"Much as we trust you, and much as we enjoy your company, there is still some need for clarification."

I could hear rustling, small cracks suggesting the snapping of twigs underfoot. My heart thundered. I thought of Ailbhe, with her swollen eye, and how I could die now in the woods without her forgiveness.

"What do you need, Seán?" I asked. "Anything.

I'll do anything."

He pulled a knife from his pocket, its blade dull in the low light, reflecting the murky forest around us.

"You'll get a head start," he said. "They're not upon us yet."

Before I could protest, his hand shot out and grabbed my wrist. Holding firm, he drew the blade along my forearm, and I felt the sharp heat of the wound as it began to throb and the rivulets of blood as they sprang forth.

"If your blood is pure, they'll spare you," he said, releasing me.

I clutched my wounded arm, staring at it mutely, pulse thundering. Seán eyed me impassively.

"If you believe your blood to be impure, I suggest you run."

Even now, I cannot say whether fear or faith held

me still to where I stood. One after the other, the wolves emerged from the thicket of trees, making themselves known. So large and ancient, their pelts heavy and dark. So beautiful that I began to weep. And the decision was made. If I was not of their blood, let me die. I didn't want to live if I wasn't among them.

One great wolf closed in on me, sniffing at my hand with curiosity, the blood running down my forearm and swelling in fat droplets at my fingertips. He licked once, smacking his chops, and retreated. His fellows followed, disappearing once more into the trees. I fell to my knees in relief, in celebration, and my body shook with joyful sobs.

All that remains is my communion. Ailbhe will come. She will witness my induction and she will understand. The work is good, and she will see it. The work is good.

AILBHE

I've been thinking a lot lately. *Ruminating*, as the therapist calls it.

The therapist is one of many people I pay to fix my problems for me. I know that's not how it works, but it's how it feels. It's how I want it to work.

It should have been easy, getting it all done. Cormac normally leaves me to go about my business. Lately I can't get rid of him. He feels guilty, I know that. He *should* feel guilty. But his response to that is to crowd me, smother me, and I feel like I don't get a moment's peace. I took another week off work and didn't tell him. Left in the mornings like usual, pretending to go about my day.

Instead I went to the therapist. Or the lawyer. Or the care home. Trying to get everything organized. Making sure I do things right. It doesn't take up much of the day. Only ever an hour here and there.

The rest of the time I find somewhere to sit, a park or the bench in a shopping centre, it doesn't matter. I sit there. Sometimes I cry. Mostly I think. I *ruminate*.

I wish I knew for sure that I was doing the right thing. The therapist assures me that I am. I wonder if she would say the same if I wasn't paying for the assurances. The lawyer says the house is Cormac's, and I agree. I wouldn't leave him with nothing. I'm not cruel. They both say the marriage is dead, the therapist and the lawyer. I don't want to agree. But maybe they're right. Maybe I'm clinging to a dead thing, hoping I can breathe life back into it. I can't love him into someone better, as my mother would say. Everyone else seems to know what to say. What do they know that I don't? How did they all get so smart?

I made one last effort at loving him better. Tried to listen, really tried. So that I could say that I put in the work. So he could never accuse me of doing otherwise. I asked him to explain it all to me and willed myself to understand. Because it would be easier to join him in this madness, whatever it is, than to leave everything behind. The things we are willing to do for a quiet life.

But I can't join him where he's going. When he spoke, it reminded me of the way the children in my class tell stories. Disjointed, meandering, and with breathless enthusiasm. I couldn't find a foothold in what he was saying, could find no way to grab on and be part of it. He was rambling. About his mother, about the Gaels of old, about modern life. I couldn't follow. I won't follow him.

I did try, though. Lord knows I tried so hard. To understand and to meet him halfway. I kissed him, held him to me as though our lives depended on it. I wanted so badly to bring him back, find any remaining sanity within him. We slept together for the first time in a long time. It was short, which was to be expected. An inelegant fumbling of limbs, still mostly-clothed. I didn't know it was over until I felt

71

him wilt inside me. We didn't disengage right away. We held fast to one another a while, lying there, my head on his chest.

"Your name means 'white rock'," he said. "You are my rock, Ailbhe."

I suppose he thought it was profound. I fought the urge to cringe. He's full of smatterings of Irish lately. Little bits here and there, mostly proverbs and words that can be translated to serve a purpose, their definitions warped.

"*Is féidir linn Gaeilge a labhairt le chéile, más mian leat,*" I said to him, his heartbeat thrumming steadily in my ear. "*B' fhéidir gur cabhróidh sé leat.*"

He was silent a moment. He won't speak Irish with me. I don't know why. I understand that he might be shy, worried about his level. But if it's as important to him as he says it is, I don't understand why he won't speak to me. I could help him if he'd let me. But it's clear he doesn't want my help.

"What if we went away?" I asked. "Lived somewhere else?"

"Like where?"

I shrugged, pulling away, rising on an elbow and off his chest. It almost felt normal. The way we used to be. Lying together and talking about the future, the promise of everything ahead of us.

"Anywhere. We could emigrate."

He rose then, and I knew I had said the wrong thing.

"We can't," he said, with finality. "Ireland will never improve if its youth keeps leaving."

And as quickly as that it was back to the same argument. The need for new blood, and the work ahead for the reclamation. Unbeknownst to him, I had done some of my own reading on the Mic Tíre. They're mad even by far-right standards. It seems their ultimate goal is total isolationism. On their website, they cite the Topographia Hibernica, a Medieval text that describes the Irish as being so isolated, so barbaric, that they could never be civilized. The Mic Tíre seem to think of this as aspirational. Would rather we return to crannogs and Brehon law, and the old ways of pre-Christian Ireland. They speak of it with all the reverence of a cult.

"Besides," Cormac said. "There's my mother to think of."

Rich coming from him. But I've thought plenty about Jacinta, especially in recent days. I've visited so many nursing homes. Only the best for her. I wouldn't leave her with anything less. Even if it bankrupts me. I told her I wouldn't leave her, but if I have to then I'll leave her in capable hands. Far from Cormac and the rabbit hole he's falling down.

The separation will be slow. It has to be, for my safety. People might think I'm being alarmist, if I could even speak to them about it. I haven't told any of my friends, not that I speak to them much lately anyway. What would I say? How could I explain away the person Cormac has become? How could anyone understand that he wasn't like this to begin with?

I've been thinking, *ruminating*, of a trip we took years ago. Before we were married. We were interrailing through the former Eastern Bloc. We'd decided to stay a while in Varna, in Bulgaria. Wetting our feet in the Black Sea while we ate at beach-side restaurants, all the sweet stray cats of the city emerging from the dark to rub at our bare ankles and beg for scraps. There were ships on the horizon, growing harder to spot as the sun continued its descent beyond the horizon. Frigates and aircraft carriers, cruising just beyond the waves.

"Imagine living here," Cormac said, bent over in his seat to scratch the head of a confident tomcat.

"I could get used to it," I replied, closing my eyes and hearing the waves lap gently at the shore.

WAX AND WANE

"We could live somewhere different every year," he said. "We've a whole planet to explore."

We had, once. He made it sound like science fiction. Like an adventure. A story you'd tell a child.

He fell asleep before me, arm still slung about my shoulders. I lay awake and kept thinking, kept ruminating. He's bringing me to a Mic Tíre event. I will go and play the role of the dutiful wife, the obliging woman. But I am always thinking, thinking, thinking.

v: full

CORMAC

Of all the days for the bus to be late. If it is late, that is. I hope we haven't missed it. We were delayed because Ailbhe had to change. I'd told her to dress nicely, that this was an important occasion and called for a bit of formality. But she still declared herself to be ready to go, still dressed in her work clothes.

"Have you nothing a bit nicer to wear?" I asked.

She held my gaze, her expression blank, before plodding up the stairs. I could hear the opening of drawers on the landing, and the rustling of cloth. It's a difficult balance. I couldn't tell her the precise nature of the event, was warned against doing so. She won't be able to witness it first hand anyway, the women are to retire to the lounge for the duration of the communion. But it's difficult to stress the importance of it all, the need for a sense of ceremony, without divulging details.

WAX AND WANE

I, myself, am clad in a suit that hasn't been worn since dad's funeral. There's a mass card still in the pocket, bearing his photo. I keep it with me. To have him there for the day that's in it. He'd be proud, I think.

Mam was asleep. There will be a mess to clean when we arrive home later, I know it, but my excitement keeps my mind from landing on such things. It isn't important, not today. I push down my resentment that mam has to factor into it at all. That she's something that needs to be taken into consideration.

Ailbhe suggested we emigrate. What a notion. I told her we couldn't, that we had a duty to mam, but I didn't mean that. Lately I can't stand to be in the same room as the woman, that overgrown infant resigned to her bed. Pissing and shitting where she lies. What good will she be when the reclamation comes? How will she contribute? The old and the infirm can only hold us back. Ireland needs new blood. She has served her country well, but not well enough. If only she'd learned Irish, taught it to me as a child. Raised me to be the soldier I am now fighting to become. She left me at such a disadvantage. Here I am, a grown man, undoing the decades of her poor parenting. She will die with the last vestiges of the modern age. She will be martyred for the rebirth of the nation. It's almost too great an honour for her.

Ailbhe came down the stairs wearing an old cocktail dress that I'd not seen her don in years. She hadn't the time to iron, the hem creased and waved unflatteringly around her knees. The fit wasn't great. Too snug about the bust, the waist riding up from the swell of her stomach. I hadn't noticed how much she'd let herself go.

"Is this good enough?" she asked.

Her face was wan. No make-up. Hair was limp, the workday having beaten the volume from it. It wasn't good enough, but then we didn't have the time to fix it. So I simply handed her her coat and moved to the door, guiding her on our way.

She stamps her feet against the cold, keeping her distance from me as we wait.

"You're awful quiet," I say. She doesn't look at me.

"I'm not feeling well," she says.

She's impossible to read of late. We finally had sex again. She actually initiated it. I think she might be breaking, accepting her place and accepting me as the man of the house. Orthodoxically speaking, it is frowned upon for the wife to initiate. It is her role to be ever yielding, to respond to the advances of the husband with loving obedience. But it is, at least, a step in the right direction. An indication that she is receptive to touch again. She still has a ways to go, but she's learning.

But her mood bothers me. Her features are settled into a loose frown, a resting state of quiet dismay. I can't keep creeping around her in respect of her feelings, nor can I keep prostrating myself before her, begging forgiveness. It's gone on too long already. I can't keep indulging her, allowing her to grow as petulant as a spoiled child.

The bus arrives and my relief rises and falls, giving way to a wave of excitement as the doors hiss open.

"Our chariot awaits," I say to Ailbhe, extending my hand for hers.

But she only gazes darkly at me, steps past me, and boards. I follow her, tossing my coins in the driver's box, swaying down the aisles to the back where she's perched herself on a seat and closed her eyes, leaning her forehead against the cool glass of the window.

"What's with you?" I ask, sitting beside her.

"I told you, I don't feel well," she says, her eyes still closed.

"The window's wet," I tell her. "You'll ruin your hair."

She doesn't budge. I notice a stain on my trousers, left by some spilled drink after dad's burial, and curse myself. I suck the air, will it to calm me against the rising tide of frustration at my slovenly suit, my slovenly wife.

"We'll be seated together at the start," I say. "After that you'll have to follow the women into the lounge."

"Can't I stay with you?" she asks.

"No. Women are not permitted in the chamber."

"Ridiculous," she mutters. "I won't know anyone there."

"You'll get to know them," I say. "They're good people, you'll like them."

She says nothing. I don't understand why she can't try harder. Especially after everything I've done this past while, trying so hard for her. A marriage is supposed to be a two-way street, but she never gives me an inch. Sometimes she pretends to. Will offer something to me, like the opportunity to converse in Irish, to help me improve. But it's only ever a veiled insult. She knows I won't accept, because if I do I open myself up to ridicule. It's the cruelty in her. It needs to be stamped out.

Abruptly, she rises from her seat, knocked about by the motions of the bus. She hits the "Stop" button on the railing and steps into the aisle.

"What are you doing?" I ask.

"I need to get off," she says, suddenly breathless.

I place my hands on her shoulders, attempt to ease her back into her seat.

"Don't be daft," I tell her. "We're already late."

"I need to get off!" she says, louder and with force. "I'm going to be sick!"

Other passengers are twisting around in their seats now to witness the scene, this humiliating display.

I bear down harder with my hands, pinning her to her seat.

"Cormac, let me go!" she cries, and some passengers even rise from their seats, uncertain as to whether or not they should intervene.

I attempt to smile at them, looking about the bus with an air of what I hope translates as amicable apologia, assuming the role of the loving husband quietening his hysterical wife. Still, they eye me with some unease, some suspicion.

The indicators click with the driver's intention to pull in at the next stop, and I grit my teeth against this unnecessary delay. Beneath my palms, Ailbhe's body is heaving, her breath rising and falling heavily in her chest. She attempts to rise again, pressing against the weight of my hands.

"Cormac, please-" she groans, before a thick stream of bile escapes her and splatters down the front of her cocktail dress through her open coat, dotting it

with specks of half-digested food and filling the bus
with a hideous acidic miasma.

AILBHE

On average, it takes seven attempts for someone to leave an abusive relationship. That's what the therapist says.

I can understand why. I can already feel the will waning, my strength being sapped from me. It's all too hard, all too much. And yet I still question if this is abuse. Am I being ridiculous, making too big a deal of everything? Am I merely seeking an exit because of Cormac's views, painting him as a worse villain to alleviate guilt? To soften the blow of accepting a failed marriage. Because a marriage can't be failed by one person alone, can it? There has to be two of us in it, doesn't there?

Is it failed or can it be salvaged yet? I suppose I only lean towards salvaging because I'm afraid to leave. There's a comfort in a certain degree of misery. Maybe I'm looking to stay on the path of least resistance. But what does that make me, then? If I stand by as he rots with all this hatred, these ideas that pour from him as though from infected sores.

I wish I could talk to someone. Someone I wasn't paying, someone impartial. But maybe bias will always exist in conversations like these. I wish someone could tell me what to think, what to do, and to make it happen. And then I realize, with uncomfortable irony, that Cormac could be that person. That he seems so keen to tell me what to do, and to have me blindly follow. I suppose I don't really want that at all. Not from him. Not after believing for so long that he loved me for the person I was, not as an extension of himself.

He wouldn't let me off the bus. I'm aware that I'm sulking, clutching to this one offense like a child would, a child having been denied their way. And I do feel so much like a child. I want to run to my mother and have her cradle me, force the weight of all these decisions on her and retreat into an infantile passivity. We sat for the duration of the journey, me stinking and splattered with the contents of myself. A kind old woman offered me some tissues with a gentle smile, and I nearly wept. Could have cried at the simple gesture. I dabbed ineffectively at the stain, but the sprawling patch of wetness still showed on the creased satin, its furthest reaches dark and stinking of bile.

We walked in silence from the bus stop to the lodge, our shoes throwing moisture from the rain-slickened road in light splashes onto our calves. He strode a pace or two ahead, better to be upwind from me. I wanted to ask how long it would be, how far we were going, but I thought better of it. I don't think he'd have answered me anyway, he was so angry.

The lodge itself is a peculiar building. Old, certainly, a long driveway winding from the gate, up the soft incline of a gentle hill towards the red-brick edifice. I imagine it had been some manner of estate once, its lands tended to by peasants in service of a distant British lord. It must have been grander then. The brickwork has crumbled in some areas. The neoclassical pillars that adorn the entrance are pocked with a peculiar rust-coloured lichen, giving the impression from afar of blood splatter.

We are guided indoors by a gaunt, suited man. It all seems a bit silly, all that pomp and ceremony. He takes our coats, drapes them over his stiffly held arm, and disappears from view to secret them someplace. We stand a moment in the foyer, the muffled sound of chatter and the clinking of glasses nearby, and look around at the sweeping staircase, the wood-paneled walls, all shining and glossed with varnish. An older man emerges from behind a heavy door, his silver hair bright in the warm light of the lodge. He smiles at Cormac.

"The man of the hour," he says, extending a hand that is excitedly accepted by Cormac.

"Seán," he says. "Sorry we're late."

The fact that he doesn't look at me feels deliberate.

A pointed absence of acknowledgement, leaving me to stand tall against the queasy guilt and dread worming through my gut.

The man, Seán, however, does look at me, before returning to Cormac.

"Your wife?" he asks.

"Ailbhe," I offer, extending my own hand.

He bows at the waist, his hand gently cupping my own, and lands a soft kiss just above my knuckles. Despite the dignity of the gesture, I notice his nose wrinkle somewhat as he nears the vomit-stained front of my dress.

I will admit that it all seems more genteel than I anticipated. None of Cormac's talk painted the picture of country estates, suits and ties, and adherence to etiquette. Especially when the group's talking points seemed so akin to the idle, inflammatory chat of any bog standard bigot down the pub.

WAX AND WANE

"Delighted to finally meet you, Ailbhe," Seán says. "I've heard so much about you."

"All good things," I say, shooting a look towards Cormac. But neither man acknowledges this contribution.

Instead, Seán gestures to the door behind him, and invites us to enter.

"Come meet everyone," he says, holding the door open for us as we enter the large room.

The ceilings are high, painted sky blue and trimmed with delicate and ornate molding in white. Around us, men and their wives chat and laugh, the men all keeping a firm hand on the lower backs of their women. They are suited, the wives in very fine gowns, and I feel myself shrink, trying to hide myself in full view, lest they see the mess that I am.

I notice, as we approach a small cluster of couples, that the women are all pregnant. Their stomachs all swell in uniform size beneath the delicate chiffon and organza of their gowns. They're radiant, their faces serene and beatific. I don't belong here.

"Cormac!" one man exclaims upon our arrival, his hand leaving his wife's body just long enough to extend in anticipation of a greeting.

He and Cormac shake hands, warmly, all the while the man's wife stares at me. She's smiling softly, but I fidget beneath her glare, uncomfortable with the intensity of it.

"And this must be Ailbhe," says the man. No hands are extended my way.

Instead, I nod bashfully, attempt to cross my arms over the stain on my dress in a way that still appears casual.

"Lovely to meet you all."

"*Fáilte*," the wife says, taking a step forward in order to place her hands on my shoulders and lean in to kiss me on the cheek.

Before I can reciprocate, she has returned to her husband's side, one hand resting on the crest of her belly. Seán taps a glass with a knife to draw the attention of the crowd, and the chatter dims to a hush.

"It is time for this evening's entertainment, if you will all follow me," he instructs.

The crowd follows him into an adjoining room, smaller and cast in darkness. There are seats arranged in neat rows, upon which all the couples perch. Before them is a screen, not yet illuminated. I follow close to Cormac, sit closer to the aisle. He still won't look at me. My hand hovers over his and I debate touching him, seeking some reassurance, but the projector comes to life and washes the screen in a pale glow and the moment passes.

We all settle back into our seats, faces turned towards the screen, and watch as a black title card flashes.

"Great Moments in Mic Tíre History," it reads.

What follows causes my stomach to lurch, folding on itself, seeking more matter to purge when there is none. Is all still clinging to my dress, to the floor of the bus. Still the heat rises to my throat and my eyes water, unable to look away from the horrors playing out on the screen. Around me, couples lean into one another, and I assume for a moment that they, too, are horrified. Turning to one another to escape the sights before them.

But then I hear that they are laughing. I see their shoulders, silhouetted by the projector's beam, quaking with mirth. A red glow is cast about the room by the wretched images on the screen, and I feel myself grow dizzy. I rise from my seat, prompting quiet hisses from those behind me. For the first time since our bus journey, Cormac looks at me. He is lit in by the crimson light of the screen, all the reliefs of his features made grotesque by the shadows. There's a warning in his eyes, one that promises violence, but

WAX AND WANE

I cannot stay.

The laughter of the crowd mingles with the guttural screams from the film and the room is brightened, if just for a moment, by my pushing through the door and out into the large reception room. Though my legs are shaking, I have to go. I have to leave.

vi: waning gibbous

CORMAC

I try to hold myself still, fight against the tremors of rage when Ailbhe rises from her seat and stands there, mute and frozen in front of the screen like a deer in headlights. She looks to me, her eyes bulging with a grotesque sheen in the low light, pleading. And in this moment I hate her, more than I ever imagined possible. Her weakness, her impudence, all her airs and graces laid bare and found to be lacking, just fragile rot slick with vomit. She is nothing. Less than nothing, and it wounds me.

Wounds me to be bound to such a woman. An unworthy vessel for the nation's future. No vessel at all. Empty. Barren. Recoiling from my touch, using her sex to manipulate me, placate me. No more. I have done my part, I have bent over backwards for her, and she has insulted me at every turn. This is her final insult.

She bolts from the room and I am glad. She

doesn't belong there. She has proven that much. We don't belong together. Ireland has greater plans for me, and where I go she cannot follow. And I will not follow her where she runs tonight. I am where I need to be. Where I have been headed my whole life. She can join the scum that is to be scrubbed from the earth.

And what great scrubbing there is. I return to the screen and gaze in awe at the work of my brothers, to whom I will be bound in communion tonight. Their powerful bodies, lithe and muscular, moving faster than their prior forms could ever allow. There is only so much a man can do in this life. Only so far he can go. A beast can do more, go further. And my brothers, how far they go.

The screams ring out in the confines of the small theatre, like a choir, each voice overlapping and adding a new layer to the beauty of what we witness. The laughter of the audience has given way to hushed admiration. We watch, enthralled, as the brothers latch their powerful jaws around the limbs and throats of men, women, children. All of them screaming, crying out to foreign gods who cannot hear them now. Their gods have no dominion here. Here, they are at the mercy of the sons of the land and their fierce justice.

I weep. Weep as I wept in the woods, from the sheer splendor of it, the pointed teeth gnashing and flaying flesh from the bone. The pleading shrieks in languages I cannot understand, that were never meant to be spoken on this island. The muzzles of the brothers are matted with blood, their snouts digging deeper into the visceral filth of the conquered. Snapping back ribs as though they were nothing more substantial than the limbs of young saplings, the quivering organs laid out before them like a hero's banquet. They feast, accept all the putrescence of those alien bodies, consume it and cleanse the earth of it. It is noble and frightening and oh, so unspeakably beautiful.

Shot after shot, scene after scene. The title card

promised great moments, and that is exactly what we receive, seated in rapture of the work. The work is good. The work is fulfilling. It lines the bellies of the brothers, clears the land for the reclamation. It warns the horde to stay away. Some say the Romans never conquered Ireland for they feared that we were giants. Let all the world think of us thus. Let them stay away for fear of the giants we are, wrapped in ancient furs, our jaws grown pointed and crowded with sharpened teeth. Let them hear our howls in the four corners of the earth, singing "Stay away, stay away, stay far away."

It takes some time for us all to register that the film has ended. Seated in the dark, our pulses drumming in unison, hearts beating the same. In joy, in fear, in anticipation of the work ahead. And though I am now without woman, it is no great mischief. I know the chapter can provide. Can furnish me with a more suitable mate. The lights come on and we all stand and applaud.

A firm hand falls on my shoulder, and I turn to see Seán smiling down upon me, haloed by the light overhead.

"I see poor Ailbhe could not stay," he says.

"No," I reply, but I feel no sorrow.

"I'm glad you are still with us" he says, and gestures for me to rise.

I comply. The communion is near at hand. We retire to the reception area for a drink, to steady my nerves. I am aware that all eyes are on me now. Normally I would shy from such attention, be suspicious of it. But tonight I am among friends. I know that they share in my excitement, in the significance of the night's ceremonies. They are happy for me, I understand. In a way that Ailbhe never could be. This is my family.

"How do you feel?" Seán asks, sipping his whiskey.

"Good," I say. "Ready."

He laughs, a low growling sound.

"Good, good," he says. "So long as you enjoy it, that's the main thing."

I nod. It begins to sink in that these are my final moments as a man, as the thing I have always been. I stand on the precipice of great change, a magnificent becoming. After tonight I will be rid of all the burdens of this life. None of it will matter anymore. The unemployment, the guilt, the shame. All will melt away in the communion, and I will be gifted a new skin. A fresh start that I never could have dreamed awaited me.

I try to pace myself, not drink too much. But the nerves eat at me, growing in number, and all I can do to quieten them is sling back drink after drink. I excuse myself to the bathroom, to splash my face with cold water. If I get too drunk, I won't be able to perform. It will be difficult enough given the circumstances, no need to make things harder for myself. I take one last look at my face. At the man I am.

When I return to the reception room, a bell is being rung. The wives embrace their husbands, then file together and depart. They are headed to the lounge, I know. The hour is upon us. Upon me. As they stream from the room, one by one, the wives smile at me. Some whisper "Good luck". My sisters. All round and full of promise, ready to populate the future. I love them all.

With the women gone, Seán approaches me.

"It's time," he says.

I follow behind him as he leads me through the lodge. The men are not far behind us. Together, we make our way to the heart of the house, which opens up into a grand atrium. It is an empty, circular space, ringed by seats with a grate at the far end. The men branch off around us, taking their places in the seats in order to get a good view. The lights are low, old, throwing only a dim amber glow. But above us, through the skylight, the moon shines bright. Seán dons his ceremonial robes, shaking them to drape comfortably over his suit. He nods to me, and I begin to undress.

A cool breeze whistles in from the skylight, coaxing my bare flesh into goose pimples. This flesh, that I have worn since infancy, that I will shed in blessed communion with my brothers. I am ready.

AILBHE

Do any of us really know anyone?

I thought I knew Cormac. I thought he was the person I knew best on all the earth. But we assume so much, don't we? Assume that proximity and duration equals knowledge. I've been close to Cormac for so long, but perhaps I never knew him at all. I certainly don't know him after tonight. After he could stomach what was on that screen.

Dear God. I don't suppose it was real? It can't be. I feel dirty. Wrong. Like I've seen something no one was meant to see. It can't have been real. Does blood really look like that? Is there so much of it? And what of those people? Surely the guards would be involved. They would have families, friends, who would go looking for them.

But the dogs. What kind of dogs were those? Massive. Like wolves, they were. But they couldn't have been wolves, there are no wolves here. They died out long ago.

My head is reeling as I traverse the long and winding drive from the manor to the gate. I shiver in the growing dark, the temperature plummeting with the sun. I didn't spare a moment to locate my coat. My arms are bare in the Autumn night, and I try to wrap myself with my own hands. Hug some warmth back into myself. And as soon as I do, I begin to cry. It wasn't supposed to be like this. It was never supposed to be like this.

How could anyone have foreseen this? Would someone else have noticed the signs? Maybe I should have paid more attention. Listened more closely. It all just sounded like the ravings of an unsatisfied man. Someone lost, and hurt, and lashing out at the world around them. My ears would have perked to anything resembling crime, wouldn't they? Or was I really so dismissive? Whatever doubts I had before, weighing pros and cons, the marriage is dead for certain now.

There is no coming back from this.

How awful it all is. Like a dream. A terrible dream.

At last I reach the gate, the dark road just beyond. I am grateful for the streetlights, their golden glow leading the way. Jesus, Cormac, how did we let it get so bad? Things were good once. I know I can't have just imagined it. There were so many dreams we shared. I don't understand. Can't wrap my head around how any of this could have happened. You never expect the bad things to find to you, safe in your little home, your little life. Who could have expected something this bad?

I let the tears fall freely as I walk. I must look a state. Not that it matters now. All that blood...I have to stop thinking about it. But every time I take a breath, allow my mind to wander, it goes back to the screen. And though I'm on the road now, the wet tarmac glistening under the lights, I am still very much in the dark room. Watching as ... it can't have been real. It was just a movie. That's why they were laughing. They were laughing at me, I bet, knowing I believed it to be real. Please let that be the case. Please let the joke be on me.

I hear something behind me, movement upon the wet road, and assume it must be Cormac. He's come to talk me down, bring me back. Wrap me in his arms and whisper assurances into my ears, all lovingly and full of affection. Anything to get me to relent. But I won't go back and he can't make me. There's no accepting what I saw back there. No explaining it away.

I pick up my pace and hear him respond in kind, his gait matching mine.

"Just leave me alone, Cormac," I call behind me, but he doesn't answer.

I'm exhausted, from the day that's in it, from the crying, and I can't keep this pace forever. I slow to a halt and before I can stop myself I'm sobbing loudly, bringing my hands to my face to shield against imagined eyes.

"Just stop, Cormac! Go back to them!"

But when I look around he isn't there. No, Cormac is not to be found, but in his stead there are three lean and mangy dogs. Their heads hung low, looking up at me with their hungry eyes. A thick strand of saliva dangles from the chops of the one in the centre, a growl shaking out from his thin chest.

I take a step away from them. They respond by stepping closer. My breath hitches in my chest and I turn, hoping that they will fall away if I pay them no heed. I try to keep myself steady, afraid that they can sense my fear, but without meaning to I feel myself accelerate, my speed kicking up a notch with each step. And with each furtive glance I shoot over my shoulder, they are gaining on me. Panic throbs in my throat, a thick lump of it, and before I know it I am jogging, my heeled shoes clacking against the road. They follow, not letting up. I kick my shoes away, my stockinged feet soaking the moisture off the ground, up through the fabric, and I run.

I can't remember the last time I've run so fast, my breath cold in my lungs, the pain of the exertion rattling my chest, stinging my face. I run and my tears cloud my vision, unable to see how far the bus stop is from me through the blur of them, and all the while the dogs follow, tireless. I can hear their panting, too close for comfort.

And now I am crying, loudly and like a child, the wails knocking out of me with each footfall. I can smell them behind me, their sodden fur, sense the hunger that lies behind the froth on their lips. And by some miracle the road intersects ahead with the slip road, the bus stop at its corner. It's so close, I am almost there, when I see the nose of the bus push into my periphery and my heart sinks. It will be at the stop before I can reach it. I will have no escape. I can't keep running, my lungs are searing and my feet are cold and wet, bloody from the force of my feet against the tarmac. I press on. Summon some strength hidden deep in the bones of me and create more distance between myself and the pack.

I get to the stop just as the driver is about to pull away. I beat against the doors with my fists, my hair wild and face red, wet with tears. He opens the doors and I slip inside, wheezing. When the bus departs, I watch with relief, a swelling sense of euphoria, as the dogs fade into the distance.

Safe, for now, I find a seat and lean against the window. It's so dark that all I can see is my own reflection. Without thinking, I pull my phone from my pocket and dial my mother's number. But as it rings, I think of how this only vindicates her, in ways that neither of us could ever have imagined. Bad as she believed Cormac to be, she could never have imagined something like this. It's beyond explanation, beyond comprehension. So as soon as I hear her voice, so surprised and delighted to hear from me after all this time, I hang up.

Will I ever be able to speak about this? Will it ever make sense enough to me? The bus presses on through the suburbs, dropping and collecting people at each stop, and I wonder what it must be like to be them instead. To be ignorant of the images I witnessed at the lodge. To live where the bad thing has yet to find me.

vii: third quarter

CORMAC

I have a new last name. I am now Cormac Mac Tíre. Son of the land. Official, marked in blood. A marriage, a union, made without Ailbhe. One that will last longer than that marriage. Something so much deeper, more significant.

The sickness will pass. That's what Seán told me. Though for now it feels like all there is. The pain and the nausea, pulling at every inch of me, knocking the air out of my chest with the intensity of it. It's just my body rearranging. Accommodating what I am becoming. It's all-consuming. Did I ever exist before the agony? All memory fades with the throbbing intensity of it. It's like being born again. Born with all the consciousness and awareness I lacked the first time around.

Ailbhe has largely left me to it. Skulking about the rest of the house, not venturing near our bedroom if she can help it. I suppose she will leave soon. She would be smart to do so. I've been told that control is an issue early on in the process. There's a flexing of new muscles, an attunement to the new flesh. It can be dangerous. Though we are done, she and I, I have still made every effort to shield her. Her time will come. She will face the consequences of her betrayal. But not yet. Let her run. Let me become strong. Everything in its right time.

I am learning patience. Lying every day on the bed, my bones breaking and building themselves anew. I watch as my skin is dappled with stretch marks, pale at first, gleaming scar tissue in the early light. As the flesh is pulled further the marks grow purple, bruise-dark, thick as tiger stripes.

My gums are bleeding. Each time I try to sleep, find refuge from the pain in those brief moments of respite, I awake to find bloody lines of drool connecting my mouth to the pillow. As the days wear on, my teeth fall out. I clutch them all in my fist, shake them like dice. There's a strange comfort in the weight of them in my hand, the rough edges that were once dug deep into my gums now grazing the flesh of my palms.

Once they're all gone I can feel my mouth rearrange itself in anticipation of my new teeth. I feel a cleft cut in the middle of my upper lip, the raw edges of skin stinging as I tongue them, tasting the sharp copper tang of blood. I can't help myself, lapping my tongue over the soft expanse of my gums, the slippery satisfaction of it. I can't remember when I last ate.

Even now, my stomach is receding, clinging tightly beneath my ribs. With each day the hunger grows more fervent. Mam will be the first, I've decided. Though the thought of her often turns my stomach, marinating in her own filth. But she's the right choice. A worthy sacrifice. Her body can carry her no further, and she'll only be dead weight when the reclamation comes. There's a pleasing symmetry to it. Having her feed me upon my new birth, as she did upon my first. I'll go for her throat first. Make it quick. No need to let her suffer. And I'll need to eat quickly, build my strength.

I imagine my jaws, how they'll stretch in front of my face, the strength of the new muscle behind them. My new teeth, all pointed and fit for purpose. The meat of her, the heat of it, and the long-awaited satisfaction. And I suppose, in her own way, she will be serving the cause. Adding fuel to the fire. Giving me the strength I need to become the footsoldier I am destined to become.

There's no more dignified end for her. She can die in squalor here, or have an honourable death. Be part of something larger, something enduring. If she could speak, I think I know what she would choose.

I just wish dad was alive to see it all. I know he would join me, old as he was. Perhaps if I'd found the pack sooner, introduced him, he might still be alive. The change breathes new life into the bones. A certain immortality, all our lives intertwined and carried in the words and memories of the collective.

They would have carried him. He'd have found a home among them, as I have. If only I'd awoken to the cause earlier.

But I suppose his death was necessary. Would I have ever ventured down this path were it not for that loss? Thank you, dad, for dying so that I might find my brothers. Thank you, mam, for the sacrifice you are about to make. For giving your body in service of my birth, as a man, then as a beast. Women like you are to be revered.

I will preserve part of you, mam. So that my future children might know you. Might understand where they came from, better than I ever did. So that my new wife can see the dimensions of a woman, a woman willing to feed the new world. Your skull, perhaps. If I can keep enough of my mind clear when in the heat of the change, I will preserve your skull. Fish out of it the rotten mind, the illness that has afflicted you for so long, and make you something worthy of reverence. I only wish I could have dad's skull as well.

A great weight pushes through the small of my back, my spine lengthening and stretching the skin to cover the new growth. Soon it will be a tail, will move as easily and mindlessly as I now blink. My knuckles retreat and rearrange beneath my skin, seeking a settlement that will accommodate all of my states.

Will I ever look entirely like myself again? I'm not sure. My brothers tell me that they were different before. Not just weaker, slighter. But imperceptibly different. They recognize it in themselves when they look at their reflections. There's an aspect of the men they were before that is lost to them now. Not something they can pinpoint precisely, something nebulous.

Coarse hairs burst through my skin, flexing and standing on end, testing the limits of each freshly sprouted follicle. I am a thing in flux. I hear the door click open every so often, by barely an inch. I know

Ailbhe must be watching. Let her see. Let her drink in the spectacle that I am, neither man nor wolf, flesh seeking equilibrium. My panting mouth, dark with blood, the cleft healing unevenly, the ever-shifting size and shape of my eyes. Let her seek the face of the man she married and find nothing. Let her quake with fear before everything she forged, the monster shaped by her neglect. Had she loved me better, things might be different. Had she joined me, life could go on.

Mam won't be enough. So frail, so insubstantial. With her consumed, I will turn to Ailbhe. Sate myself on the old life. Why spare her? It's only prolonging the inevitable. Better to kill her soon, gorge myself on the flesh she so callously denied me, and be done with it.

My spine bends and my eyes water from the pain of it all. It is almost at an end. Fissures form along my stretch marks, the skin bursting, unable to contain the growth within. Goodbye, goodbye. I'll see you all on the other side.

AILBHE

I'm pregnant.

I sit atop the toilet seat, the test held between my fingers, and stare in disbelief at the twin lines. I try to cast my mind back, count through the months, identify when this could have happened.

Before Jasper. We'd been together not long before she died. Before Cormac killed her. And that was just over two months ago now, wasn't it? I hadn't noticed the missed period. I've been so tired. And since the lodge it's only gotten worse. It's as though the dogs followed Cormac home. They've stationed themselves at the gate again, howling the entire night through. More of them, now. Growing in number every night. I can't even be sure if I have slept. Sometimes I think I have, but everything seems to bleed together. There's a haze about it all, like nothing is quite real.

Am I really pregnant at all?

WAX AND WANE

I pinch my thigh, feel the pain. Watch as the whitened patch of skin grows pink, the blood returning. I'm awake. I'm pregnant.

Were things different, were they normal, he would be so happy. After all, this is everything he'd been hoping for. Everything I'd denied him. And how right I was to deny him, now that I know the full extent of it. How far gone he is. How dangerous. No one could bring a child into that. Yet here I am. Wondering what to do. What happens next.

One thing is certain, Cormac cannot know. It's a secret I'll keep folded inside of me, nestled among the organs. He'll have to cut it out of me to know. I shudder at how real that possibility now seems.

Would he really hurt me? Hurt me like those families in the video? More than the black eye he already left. Something more permanent next time. Frightened as I've been this whole time, I haven't allowed myself to really believe in the danger. Some sentimental part of me still thinks the love will protect me, spare me. But it isn't enough, never was. The love wasn't enough to steer him off this path, and he's much too far gone now. If I stay, I believe I'll die.

I have a bag, largely packed. Cormac has been resigned to the bedroom for days, unaware of my movements. But I'm stuck on finding ways to get Jacinta out. I can't take her with me. She cannot walk, and would slow me down. I understand how cruel that sounds. I won't leave her to be harmed by him, though. She can't be admitted to a nursing home without Cormac's consent, I've already tried. But I hope that by calling an ambulance when I leave, that someone will come and see the care that she so desperately needs. Will be able to help her in ways that I can't, couldn't.

The guilt crushes me. Makes it hard to breathe. There are so many things I wish I could do differently, but that luxury simply isn't mine. I sit by Jacinta's bed and stroke her hand. Her face is still, eyes only on me.

WAX AND WANE

"Can I tell you a secret, Jacinta?" I ask.

"Wuhh-wuh-," she says, and I almost burst into tears right then.

It's the closest to a word she's managed in months. I can taste the question in the air. The "What?" she wants so desperately to voice. I clutch her hand in my own. Already so cold.

"I'm pregnant," I say, and just saying it aloud shakes the tears loose.

I don't know what response I was expecting, but when Jacinta's eyes grow wide and chill with fear I am taken aback. Her hand is shaking in mine.

"Wuhh," she groans. "Wuhhhehhh."

My brow notches in confusion, in an effort to decipher her meaning. She can't have been asking a question before. Stupid of me to assume. I hold onto her as she fights the tide of illness, labours to form her mouth around the sounds she needs to make. But I can see that the strength is already leaving her, that the endeavour is exhausting her.

"You can do it, Jacinta," I whisper. "I'm here. I'm listening. You can do it."

But she merely exhales a faint "Wuhhh" before her hand slackens in mine. I brush the hair from her brow. She turns her eyes from me. I want so badly to understand. Jacinta would understand me too. She's been here the whole time, has been aware of what's been going on in her own way. She's my only advocate.

Her eyelids grow heavy, lashes fluttering, and I know to leave her. Let her get her rest. Des would be furious to see how bad things have gotten. He never would have allowed Cormac to get like this, would have beaten it out of him if he needed to. He was a good man, was Des. He and Jacinta were good parents, I'm sure of it. They've been great in-laws to me, always treated me like their own. Their hearts would break if they knew what Cormac was becoming.

WAX AND WANE

My own heart breaks, in the few moments I can allow myself to crack the door open and peek in at him. I tell myself at first that I do it only to know how much time I have left. How long it will be before he has the strength to leave the room. But I know that I'm drawn by a morbid fascination too. Each time I look, my brain rejects the sight of him. Has no way to make sense of it. This great, pulsating thing, its form shifting fluidly. Painfully, too, it sounds like. I hear him at all hours, gasping and groaning against it all.

The fear barely registers. He's too foreign a thing to fear. An abstract lifeform, a lump of clay being molded by unseen hands. I watch him and wonder again if I'm truly awake. But I know that not even my dreams could conjure such sights.

I could kill him now, I think, while he's still weak. The thought is so sudden, so invasive, that I bring a hand to my mouth in shock. Did I really think that? The exhaustion makes me feel like someone else. Like I've the mind of someone else, floating parallel with my own. But it's right, isn't it? I could kill him. Kill it, whatever it is he's becoming, while he's vulnerable and writhing on our bed. If he is something that can be killed, that is. I can't be sure.

I rest a hand on my belly. Is it your voice, I wonder? The thing inside of me? Are these your thoughts? Maybe you're trying to protect me, protect both of us by spurring me to do things I never thought possible. But I'm not sure that it's you. Not sure that I want you. You don't exist. Not yet. Not in any real sense. But I do. I exist. I'm here. I'm awake. There's something liberating in that knowledge, simple as it is.

I'm awake. I can decide what happens next.

I close the door, leave Cormac to his agony. And I am thinking, thinking, thinking. How do you kill an unnatural thing? A thing that shouldn't be? There's still enough of man about him that he can be killed, surely. He can't escape his humanity entirely. And a man is something I can kill.

WAX AND WANE

Time is scarce. I push my weight behind one chest of drawers, moving it in front of the bedroom door. It won't hold him, not for long, but it will be enough.

viii: waning crescent

CORMAC

I can feel her in me now. All her memories, her words. See Ireland as it was and can be again. My breathing is shallow, fur wet with viscera, the old skin still sliding away in uneven lengths. My body submitted to the light of the moon, its gravity ripping meat from bone as easily as it pulls at the tides. I split away from myself, reassembled, was born anew. Now I am bloody and weak as an infant, lying still as the strength pulses through me. Some measure of her power, old as the land itself.

As soon as I was nude and ready, standing in the atrium, Seán had made his way to the grate at the far end of the room. He pulled on a pair of thick leather gloves and drooped to grab and pull the rusted grate away, revealing a dark tunnel leading from where we had all gathered. He fished a hand around in the dark, eventually finding what he was seeking, and wrenched sharply. From the within the dark, I heard a yelp.

He pulled again, really putting his back into it, feeding a length of chain through his hands. Gradually, the beast emerged, fighting against Seán's might but losing. Large as she was, larger than any of my brothers, she was weak. Ancient. Her eyes were clouded, blue and swirling as the Milky Way. Dust wafted from her dull coat, rust red and matted. She was lean, bore a hungry and pathetic look, and wheezed into the arena.

"Behold the Morrigan," Seán announced, to the spellbound appreciation of the men seated around us.

"Guardian of the land. Harbinger of death. Shapeshifting goddess of ages past."

The Morrigan twitched her head about, sniffing the air, her great shoulders shifting. Even in that weakened state, her power was undeniable. A living relic of the days of old, when the veil between the worlds of man and sidhe was thin.

Seán had earlier explained everything to me, of course, but it was another thing entirely to see her in the flesh. The flesh that had trapped her for millennia. We've moved so far beyond the Ireland she knew. The modern age has dulled the power the land once held. Formed too strong a barrier between the worlds. She can no longer change. Is imprisoned within the pelt of the red wolf, a pelt she donned when she did battle against Cú Chulainn. And who was Cú Chulainn but a brother of ours, in all but name? Were his warp spasms so different from our own changes, the wrenching transformations of our anatomies?

What a thing it is, to commune with a god. Naked in the moonlight, I approached her, my hands before me so she could find the scent of me. She bucked, backing away, but Seán held her firm, the chain wrapped around his fist. I extended a hand, meaning to place it upon her enormous head, but her jaws snapped at the air, seeking to bite me. The men all laughed.

WAX AND WANE

"You'll want to approach her from behind," instructed Seán. "Try not to get bit until the deed is done."

I closed my eyes, steadied my nerves. Tried to pretend the men were not there, were not watching. I moved behind the Morrigan, one hand on my cock, stroking it into attention. She knew what was about to happen. Had endured it with each of my brothers. She fought against the chain, thrashing her head about, yanked back into place again and again by Seán's steady hand.

I tried not to think of Ailbhe. Tried to replace her with any other woman my mind could conjure. Some nameless, faceless figure, feminine and pleasing. But Ailbhe always returned. The fullness of her, the warmth of her against me. The scent of her as I inhaled, her wetness on the tips of my fingers, the heat of her breath in my ear as I bore into her. Ailbhe who I had loved so much once. A pang of sorrow pierced my chest and was quickly muted by anger. By the knowledge that the life with Ailbhe was over, and the fault lay with her. That all the bodily pleasures of her had been denied me, would only continue to be denied, and that there was nothing left for me within her.

I grabbed a handful of the Morrigan's red fur, my fingernails bearing down into her haunches. My hand kept working, coaxing myself into readiness, thinking of the women in the video. Their screams, their undoing. How quickly and easily the flesh yielded. Once hard enough, I pressed myself against the Morrigan, found her entry. She barked, body vibrating with growls beneath me, but I held fast. I wrapped my arms around her, holding her in place, squeezing against her ribs. As I panted, eyes clamped shut, Seán must have released the chain.

I clung to the beast as she thrashed, seeking to shake me loose, and I could feel myself growing closer. Thinking of the flesh and the work ahead. The glory that would come. And soon I was coming, the force of it shaking through my legs. In my ecstasy my grip upon the Morrigan loosened, just enough for her to turn and catch my arm between her powerful jaws. She bit down hard and I screamed, spilling blood and semen on the dirt floor of the atrium.

Seán took up the chain again and pulled the beast back into submission. I doubled over on the ground, each nerve in my body thrumming with pain and pleasure. The bite was deep. Deep enough to send her coursing through my veins, already changing me. The men stood from their seats and applauded.

"Welcome, Brother Cormac Mac Tíre," Seán said, the Morrigan still sniffing the air blindly, her angry mouth hungry for more of my blood.

I am her son now. Infected with her. My new eyes attune to the moonlight and I can see countless nights like this, stretching back over all the ages. I am her. I am the land. All its memories etched deep in my bones. I see the lives of my brothers, too. And they can see mine, I know. Can feel the grief and the sorrow I endured. What a relief it is to share it among the pack. To have it scattered across time and space, no longer weighing upon me.

I ease up onto my four legs, the bed creaking beneath my weight. I can taste my mother on the air. My first mother. Jacinta. Can hear the steady drumming of her pulse. The hunger is upon me, I am mad with it, my maw dripping with thick ribbons of saliva. I've fasted so long. It is now my time to feed.

Ailbhe, too, is nearby. I really thought she would have left by now. She is either more brave or more stupid than I realized. I have hunger enough for them both. And all of that fullness of Ailbhe, her heat and her flesh, it seems so appealing again. So ripe and ready for me. Offer yourself to me, Ailbhe, one last time. Be a wife to me again. Let me have you, destroy you, and be the man you never allowed me to be.

I rise from the bed and approach the door, pushing

against it with my great heft. It holds firm. Something is blocking the way from the landing. Perhaps Ailbhe is smarter than I gave her credit for. Has she stayed to fight? Is she so naive to think she can kill me now that I have become so much greater? Not to worry. I have new strengths to be tested. Here is my first challenge. Get out of the room. Find her.

AILBHE

It's time to leave.

I'm trying to lift Jacinta from her bed, struggling to get her somewhere safe with me, when I hear the bedroom door begin to batter against the chest of drawers. He'll be out soon. I knew taking Jacinta would be a risk, that it would slow my escape, but at the last minute I simply couldn't leave her. I knew it wouldn't be right.

I drape her arm across my shoulders, try to balance her weight across me. She's still in her nightgown, legs bare, but I've no time to dress her in anything warmer. There's a loud crack, the doorframe splitting against the force of Cormac's shoving. Jacinta is trembling, her limbs limp and finding no purchase, unable to walk.

"Wuuuhhh," she moans.

"I know," I say. "I know. It's OK, we're getting out."

I try to take a step forward but it's so hard beneath her dead weight. I struggle to find my balance, push forward.

"Wuuuhhhheehhhhhhh," she says, but I keep pushing on, sweat already beading on my brow.

The door of our bedroom, mine and Cormac's, is reduced to splinters. I see them burst out across the landing, littering the carpet. We're done. He'll be out and upon us in no time. My knees begin to buckle and Jacinta's arms slide from my shoulders, her body drooping to the ground. I fall with her, the two of us tangling and collapsing as the chest of drawers is violently pushed across the landing, the joints of the wood knocking loose in the process.

"Wuhhhehhdd," Jacinta cries, eyes wild and brimming with tears. "Wuhhedding! Wedding!"

But I'm not listening to her now, can't hear anything beyond the low growling of the thing that emerges from my bedroom, its rust-red fur bristling on end, making itself look so much larger and more menacing. It sniffs the air, its snout wrinkling back into a snarl, lips retreating to offer a view of its long teeth. As it approaches, I see its eyes, and find no part of Cormac in them. He is gone, well and truly, and a great cry breaks its way from my mouth. I scream in the face of this beast, in sorrow, in anger, my throat aching with the force of it.

Beyond the windows of Jacinta's bedroom, the dogs howl in the street. A great chorus of them, and I can only imagine how many of them there are now. Ten, maybe twenty. And more joining their ranks all the time. They have come for Cormac, to witness him. And Cormac now joins their call, throws back his lupine head and emits a loud and mournful howl.

"Wedding!" Jacinta shouts, close enough to my ear that I can hear her over the din of the dogs.

Her gaze bores into mine, so urgent and insistent, and at last I understand. What she's been trying to tell me for days. She knows what Cormac has become. She knows the danger we are in. And all this time she's known what to do, but has been unable to do it herself. Held back by the disease that has taken so much from her.

Wedding.

My mother didn't attend the wedding. Said she couldn't in good conscience see me marry Cormac. That morning, as I dressed, I fought a losing battle against my own tears. What should have been a happy day felt like another betrayal. Like I was again loving a man at the expense of my relationship with my mother. My mind swam with doubts and apprehensions, and for a moment I indulged the thought of running. Of leaving Cormac at the altar.

Jacinta had knocked lightly on the door. I had asked everyone else to depart, the bridesmaids, the photographer, the hairstylist. I needed air, to be on my own. Really needed to take a hard look at myself and ask if this was what I wanted. Jacinta knocked again.

"Come in," I'd said.

In her hands, she held a small box, which she passed to me without a word. I opened it to reveal a set of fine cutlery, gleaming silver.

"Oh Jacinta," I said. "They're lovely."

"They belonged to my grandmother," she said. "Given to her on her wedding day. And then to every girl in the family on her wedding day since."

My eyes began to tear and she guided me into an embrace.

"Hush now, you'll ruin your make-up," she said, clutching me tightly.

I laughed, wiping gently at my eyes, and we pulled away.

"They're real silver," she said. "It's not much, but it's the best we have."

"It's perfect," I said.

It's perfect.

Where are they now? In some cupboard in the kitchen, I imagine. The knives still sharp, the silver polished and ready. But Cormac looms in the doorway, lowering his muzzle after his lengthy howl, and his sights are set on us. If I'm quick, I can slide beneath him, get onto the landing. But that leaves Jacinta on her own to face him, and I can't have that. I won't let him get her. She pats my hand gently, urging me to make my move. To do anything. We can't cower on the bedroom floor forever.

Cormac is poised to spring forward, leaning into his hind legs, but before he can launch himself I keep low to the ground and rush under his belly, feeling his fur brush the back of my neck. I'm out, onto the landing, and with his new size it takes him a moment to react, to see where I've gone. Jacinta lies before him, he could just as easily take her now, rip out her throat before coming after me. It wouldn't even give me much of a head start. If I'm to save either of us, I need to distract him.

I pull at his tail, try to get him to whip around, to go after me instead. To spare Jacinta. But he doesn't even flinch, his body lowering to the ground, shaking with a growl, and readying to attack the elderly woman. I pull and I hit and I scream, hoping for any reaction, but he can't be distracted from his prey now that he's locked onto it.

"Cormac!" I cry, and my body is shaken with a sudden bout of sobs. "Cormac, I'm pregnant!"

The beast stops in its tracks, its tail lowers and tucks between its hind legs a moment. It whines, a sad sound, and turns its head towards me. Maybe I only make myself believe it, but I think in that moment that I see something of Cormac in its eyes.

"I'm pregnant," I say. "I'm not keeping it."

And now the beast is enraged, its hackles up, lips retreating and showing the snapping teeth again. It winds its large body around, doubling back on itself to turn on me, turning its back on Jacinta. The stairs are blocked by the chest of drawers, toppled and falling apart from being thrown across the landing. I'm upon them before I can second-guess myself, climbing over the ruined furniture and sliding over the top until my feet find a step just beyond. Cormac barks, the edges of it sharp with an ever-increasing growl rattling his bones.

My feet tumble down the stairs and I feel weightless, the adrenaline numbing me to all sensation. I roll on an ankle and feel nothing, keep bounding down the stairs, and hear the deafening thud of the beast's body landing upon the chest of drawers, following close behind. I round the end of the stairs, pass through the short hallway to the kitchen, where my eyes swivel in their sockets, seeking the cupboard that holds the silverware.

Cormac moves down the stairs with such speed that he crashes against the wall, still not fully in control of his new ungainly limbs. I open a cupboard by the sink, rifle through it desperately, but find nothing. Cormac is collecting himself, righting himself, and stalking towards me. He's enjoying this, I realize. The chase. My fear.

What did I ever do to deserve this? All I did was support him, exhaust myself trying to keep us both afloat, treading water. I loved him and gave him all of me and it wasn't enough. Still won't be enough. He will kill me tonight and it won't end with me. The full weight of the past year hits me. Everything I've done to keep the marriage together. Everything that's failed. And I remember where the cutlery is.

Cormac leaps into the kitchen and I have just seconds to launch myself away from him, sliding on the tiles. I crash against a cabinet, hitting my shoulder, and I hiss from the pain of it. I pull open the cabinet doors and there it is, the box Jacinta gave me on my wedding day, hidden away among old photo albums. Cormac had spoken idly of pawning them once, a few months after he'd stopped looking for work. I wouldn't allow that to happen.

I pull the box free, open it just as Cormac comes flying in a pounce towards me, his jaws open and ready to snap shut as he lands. I attempt to jerk out of his way, knocking the box as I do, and the silverware scatters across the floor. He's almost upon me, falling over me, the great bulk of his form all I can see. I reach around madly, trying to grab any utensils my hands land upon. I grasp something, not even seeing it, and thrust upwards. Blindly, desperately, instinctively.

He falls on top of me, and I feel that this is it. I am enveloped by the russet fur, pressed beneath his weight, and I feel him emit an enormous sigh. His lungs don't inflate again. I realize that my fist is still clutching, white-knuckled, to the silver utensil which is buried in his side. I pull it out, releasing a torrent of blood which cascades across the kitchen tiles. His body still upon me, I feel him shrink, the hair receding into the skin. He dies before he is fully himself, his corpse a grotesque halfway point between man and beast. Lying atop me, he is no longer my husband.

I am soaked in his blood when I push him aside, and I notice that I am bleeding too. Between my legs, a red stain is spreading, joined by a searing pain in my abdomen. I know at once what is happening.

Maybe our marriage was too full of secrets, things unspoken. They piled up and strained against the confines of it, tore us apart from the inside. Now something is tearing inside me, unable to survive the strain of it all. I lie beside Cormac, shimmy out of my wet clothes, and stay there until it passes. I gaze at the ceiling and am surprised that I feel nothing. Just an empty malaise.

Once the pain has ebbed away, once the cold of the tiles is intolerable, I sit up. On the floor, lying in the pool of its parents' blood, is a tiny mass. It doesn't move, it is almost certainly dead. But as I place it in my palm, I can see its little body. Everything looks so similar at that stage. Mammalian fetuses are so hard to distinguish early on. I know it is human – was to be human. Yet in the darkness, the delicate wet skin cast in the gloom, uncertainty bites at me. What would you have been?

I walk into the garden without dressing, only the blood to hide my modesty. I go to the hole where Jasper lay, where the dogs found her, and kneel in the dirt. I place the small thing, the lupine fetus, into the ground and cover it with dirt. And I think of the lodge, and all the pregnant women within it, all the men like Cormac, and the families in the video. I think of them all, and what lies ahead, and weep until the moon sets.

Saoirse Ní Chiaragáin is an Irish writer living in Berlin, Germany. Her work has previously appeared in anthologies from Ghost Orchid Press, Urhi Publishing, Pulse Publishing and elsewhere. She enjoys dive bars and jukeboxes, and worries a lot. You can follow her on Twitter @MiseryVulture. To read more of her published work, and get information on upcoming publications, visit her website - *saoirsenichiaragain.com*